SPECIAL GIFTS

THE • COBBLE • STREET • COUSINS

SPECIAL GIFTS

CYNTHIA RYLANT

illustrated by

WENDY ANDERSON HALPERIN

ALADDIN PAPERBACKS

New York London Toronto Sydney Singapore

First Aladdin Paperbacks edition September 2000

Aladdin Paperbacks
An imprint of Simon & Schuster
Children's Publishing Division
1230 Avenue of the Americas
New York, NY 10020

Also available in a Simon & Schuster Books
for Young Readers hardcover edition

Designed by Heather Wood

The text for this book was set in Garth Graphic.
The illustrations were done in pencil and watercolor.

Manufactured in the United States of America

22 24 26 28 30 29 27 25 23 21

The Library of Congress has cataloged the hardcover edition as follows:

Rylant, Cynthia.
The Cobble Street Cousins : special gifts / Cynthia Rylant;
illustrated by Wendy Anderson Halperin.—1st ed.
p. cm.
Summary: Nine-year-old cousins Rosie, Lily, and Tess spend their winter vacation learning to sew with their neighbor Mrs. White and preparing for a special winter solstice dinner with Aunt Lucy and her boyfriend Michael.
ISBN-10: 0-689-81714-2 (h.c.)
[I. Cousins—Fiction. 2. Aunts—Fiction. 3. Winter—Fiction.] I. Halperin, Wendy Anderson, ill. II. Title. III. Title: Special gifts.
PZ7.R982Cj 1999d [Fic]—dc21 98-19563 CIP AC
ISBN-13: 978-0-689-81715-1 (Aladdin pbk.)
ISBN-10: 0-689-81715-0 (Aladdin pbk.)

1014 OFF

TABLE OF CONTENTS

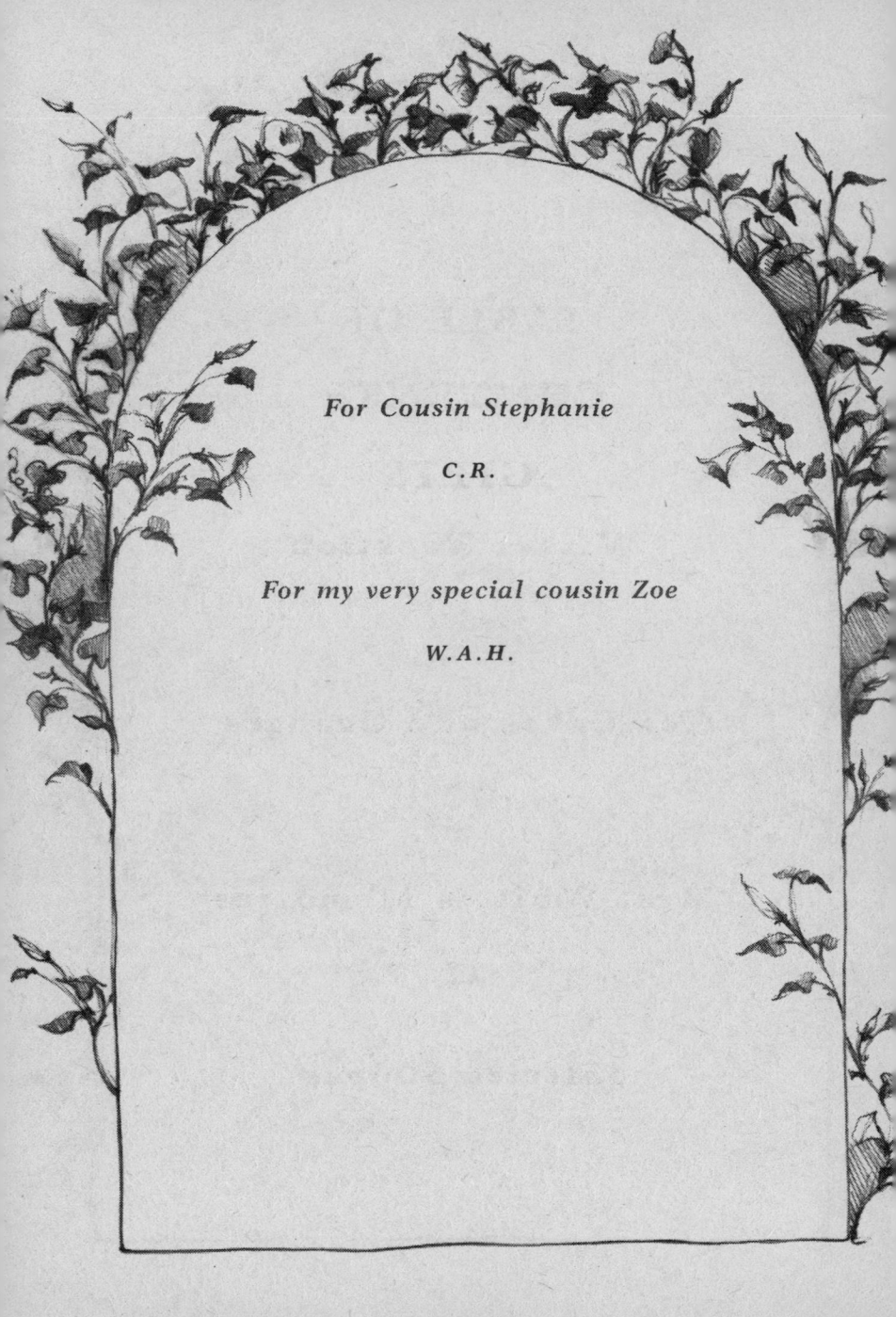

For Cousin Stephanie

C.R.

For my very special cousin Zoe

W.A.H.

SPECIAL GIFTS

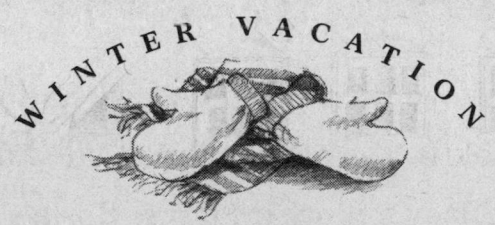

WINTER VACATION

Lily, Rosie, and Tess—all nine years old—lived with their Aunt Lucy in a lovely blue house on Cobble Street. Lily and Rosie were sisters, Tess was their cousin, and Aunt Lucy was aunt to everyone. The girls' parents all danced with the ballet, and while the ballet toured the world for a year, the cousins were sharing Aunt Lucy's attic.

It was wonderful. Each girl had her own little nook in the attic: Lily's bed was behind the long, lacy yellow curtains; Rosie's bed was behind the old patchwork quilt; and Tess's bed

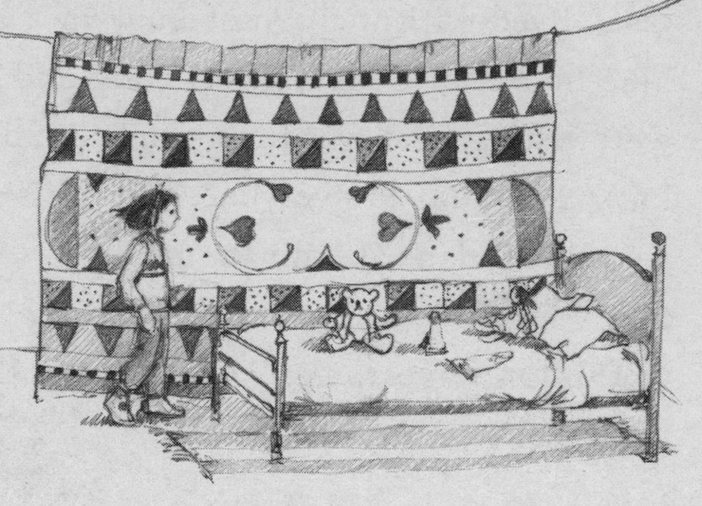

was behind the screen decorated with palm trees. The girls loved their special places, and when they all wanted to be together, they came out into The Playground—a big pile of blankets and books and toys in the middle of the room.

It was in The Playground where they began discussing Winter Vacation. Soon school would be out for three weeks. What would they do for fun?

"I suggest we learn to ice-skate," said Tess, stroking her cat, Elliott, in her arms. Tess wanted to sing on Broadway someday, and she looked for any opportunity to perform—even if it meant performing falls on ice.

"Oh no," said Rosie. "I couldn't. I'm clumsy, I'm shy, and I hate cold fingers." (Rosie loved most being quiet and warm and at home.)

"You're not clumsy," said Lily. "But you're right, Rosie, you do hate cold fingers. And I, for one, hate a sore bottom, which is exactly what I'd have if I tried to ice-skate."

"You girls are *so* unadventurous!" said Tess.

"Pain does not equal adventure," said Lily.

"Well then, what ideas do you have?" asked Tess.

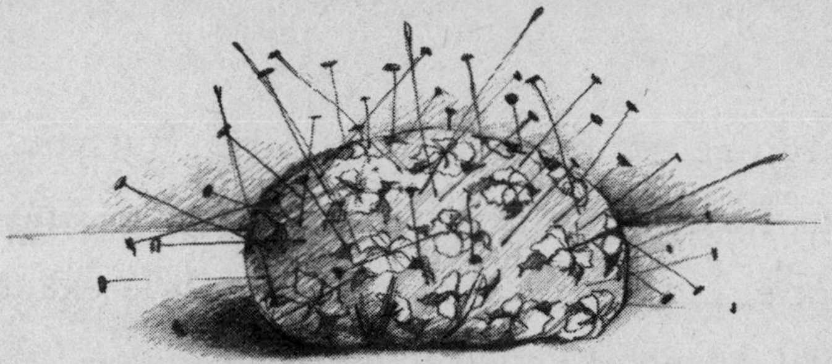

"Hmmm," said Lily, who loved ideas and coming up with them. (She hoped to be a writer someday.) "Maybe we could learn to do something less cold and painful. How about sewing?"

"I'd love to learn to sew!" exclaimed Rosie.

"Ugh," said Tess. "Boring."

"If you learn to sew, Tess," said Lily, "you can make your own costumes. You can make capes and skirts and—"

"You're right!" said Tess. "But where do we learn to sew?"

"At Mrs. White's house, of course," said Lily.

"Of course!" said Rosie and Tess.

Mrs. White was a very elderly woman the cousins had met in the summer when they delivered cookies to her on her ninetieth birthday. Since then, she had become their friend and they often stopped in to see her and chat. And whenever they visited, Mrs. White gave each of them a little cat she had sewn herself.

"I'd love to make some cotton dolls with dresses," said Rosie.

"I'd love to make a vest—with sequins," said Tess.

"I could make little pillows and decorate them with words," said Lily. "Like 'WISH.'"

"'WISH'?" said Tess. "That's all?"

"That's *everything*!" said Lily.

"What could we do for Mrs. White in return?" asked Rosie.

"I don't know," said Lily. "Let's ask her."

"And we have to ask Aunt Lucy," reminded Tess.

"Oh, Aunt Lucy will love the idea," said Lily. "She loves everything."

It did seem that Aunt Lucy loved everything. She certainly loved having the three girls live with her in her big, old-fashioned house. Aunt Lucy was young and pretty. She had long red hair and freckles and she wore the most wonderful clothes—jumpers covered with sunflowers, perky antique hats, shiny yellow lace-up boots. She owned a flower shop on the corner—Lucy's Flowers—and the cousins loved to visit her there. They drank tea and talked with the customers.

Their favorite customer, of course, was Michael Livingston, Lucy's boyfriend. The cousins had met Michael first and had introduced him to Aunt Lucy, and they were quite proud of their matchmaking. Michael lived nearby in an elegant apartment building owned by his wealthy family, and he was studying to be a botanist. The cousins all looked forward to the day he and Aunt Lucy would marry.

"Let's go to the flower shop and tell Aunt Lucy of our idea right now," said Rosie.

"We'll tell her we'll sew something just for her," said Lily.

"Like a *wedding* dress!" said Tess.

Giggling with excitement, the cousins bounded down the attic steps and went to find Aunt Lucy.

TEA CAKES AND ORANGES

With cups of lemon tea and ginger cookies in hand, the cousins sat on stools and talked to Aunt Lucy of their sewing idea while she arranged flowers. Aunt Lucy's flower arrangements were always so beautiful—"wild and windswept," Lily had called them dramatically. The girls loved to watch Aunt Lucy work.

"I think it's a wonderful idea," said Aunt Lucy, brushing a wisp of hair from her eyes as she sorted and arranged. "And Mrs. White will be so glad for the company."

"I'm going to make cotton dolls with dresses," said Rosie. "And I want all the dresses to look like yours, Aunt Lucy."

"Why, thank you, Rosie. If you master doll dresses, maybe soon you can make dresses for yourself. At least some pretty jumpers."

"I'd *love* that!" said Rosie.

"Not me," said Tess, biting into a cookie. "I live to shop."

"Tess, you sound like a bumper sticker," said Lily.

"I get my best lines from bumper stickers," said Tess.

"Ugh," said Lily.

"Why don't you girls take something to Mrs. White?" said Aunt Lucy. "I'll give you some money and you can stop in French's Market for some tea cakes and oranges."

"'Tea cakes and oranges,'" said Lily. "What beautiful words. I'm going to put them on a pillow."

The cousins said good-bye to Aunt Lucy and walked over to Maple Street to French's

Market. They all liked Mr. French. Especially Tess, because Mr. French always asked her to sing.

"Yes and how are my most favorite cousins today?" asked Mr. French when the girls walked up to the store. He was outside, brushing some snow off the awning.

"We're great, Mr. French," said Tess. "And how are you?"

"Magnificent!" he said. Mr. French had a black mustache and dark sparkling eyes and he truly seemed magnificent.

"Rosie, are you still sweet?" he asked.

"Yes," said Rosie with a grin.

"Lily, are you still wise?" he asked.

"Yes." Lily grinned as well.

"And Tess," said Mr. French, "are you still the best singer in town?"

"Yes!" said Tess.

"Then sing me a little song!" said Mr. French.

Tess grinned and cleared her throat. Then she sang a few verses from "I Love Paris."

"Outstanding!" Mr. French clapped. Lily and Rosie clapped, too. A few people in the store were looking at Tess, but she didn't mind. She loved an audience.

"We have to buy some tea cakes and oranges now," said Lily to Mr. French. "We're taking them to Mrs. White."

"Then please tell her hello for me," said Mr. French. "And tell Mary at the cash register that I said to give each of you a free pumpkin bar."

"Yum," said Lily. "Thank you, Mr. French."

When the cousins finally arrived at Mrs. White's house, a light snow was falling. The little pink house looked so cozy and warm.

"I love visiting Mrs. White," said Rosie. "She makes things so homey."

"She's had ninety years of practice," said Tess.

"I hope I'm just like her when I'm old," said Rosie.

"You're just like her *now*, Rosie," said Lily.

Rosie giggled.

The three cousins rang the bell and waited.

It always took Mrs. White a while to come to the door. But when it opened, she was always there with a smile on her face. And today was the same.

"It's the cousins!" said Mrs. White, her wrinkled skin pink and pretty, her blue eyes bright.

"It's us, Mrs. White," said Lily. "We've brought tea cakes and oranges and an idea."

"Lovely!" said Mrs. White. "I'm ready for all three! Do come in."

And the cousins stepped inside the warm little house, where they hoped to learn to sew.

MAIL

Mrs. White's Memories

It wasn't long before Lily, Rosie, and Tess were spending every other afternoon at Mrs. White's house. And they were having so much fun. They'd gotten lots of fabric scraps from Aunt Lucy and Mrs. White. Mrs. White even supplied all the needles and thread. The only thing each girl had to buy was a set of tiny sewing scissors.

They loved their scissors, for when closed, the scissors formed the head and body of a crane.

"Why don't we have such pretty scissors at school?" said Lily one afternoon in Mrs. White's kitchen. "I'd learn so much better if school had *pretty* things."

Tess giggled.

"Can you imagine going to the school cafeteria and having tea and little finger sandwiches for lunch?" she said.

"I'd love it!" said Rosie.

"When I'm finished with school, I'm never going to use anything ordinary again," Lily said. "Every bowl and plate, every bar of soap—*everything*—will be unique!"

"That's what makes sewing so nice," said Mrs. White, happily watching the girls make their little stitches. "Everything you sew is one-of-a-kind."

"I love sewing," said Lily. "And I'm so glad you're having us make pillows first, Mrs. White. That's exactly what I wanted to make."

"Well, they're simplest for learning," said

Mrs. White. "Once you feel comfortable making stitches, you can make other things."

"Like vests," said Tess.

"And dolls," said Rosie.

"Exactly," said Mrs. White.

The girls stitched happily a while longer, then it was time to take a break and continue

helping Mrs. White with the small favor they'd promised. She had a large trunk full of many things she'd saved over the years—photos, letters, small mementos—and she had asked the cousins' help in sorting it. She had a grandson who would inherit the trunk and its contents someday, and she wanted everything to be tidy.

The girls followed her into her bedroom to open the trunk at the foot of the bed. Mrs. White's bedroom was dark and quiet, with an old mahogany bed and chifforobe, a small maple writing desk, and several antique china plates on the walls. Rosie loved it, of course.

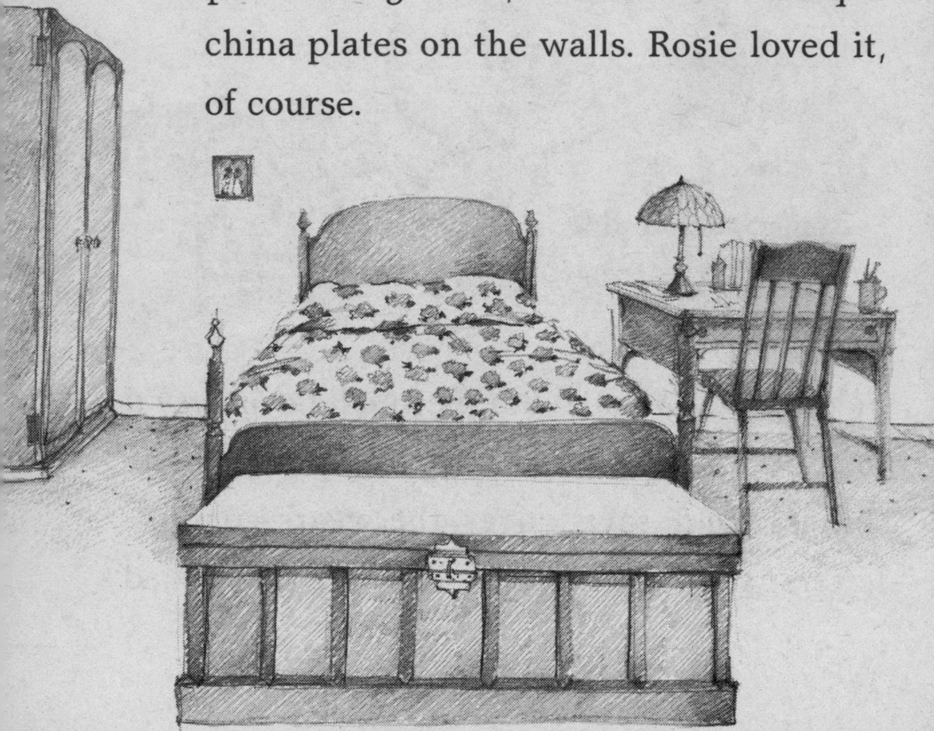

Mrs. White settled herself in a wicker armchair near the trunk as the cousins opened the lid.

"I'm so happy for your help with this," said Mrs. White. "Bending is rather difficult for me."

"Oh, we like it, Mrs. White," said Tess. "And it's easy."

"Well, I do thank you," said Mrs. White.

The cousins had already helped Mrs. White with a large number of loose old photos. They were now nicely displayed in a new album, with little notes describing what or who was in the picture.

Today the girls would help Mrs. White sort her old letters. Some were tied up in bundles, others were loose and scattered, all were yellowed with time.

"I saved letters from only two people," said Mrs. White. "My husband and Mrs. Roosevelt."

"What was your husband's name?" asked Rosie.

"Did you say *Mrs. Roosevelt*?" asked Tess.

Mrs. White smiled.

"My husband's name was Charles," she said. "And yes, my friend was Mrs. Roosevelt. Eleanor Roosevelt."

"Oh, my gosh!" said Tess. "I saw a movie about her. She was *famous*!"

"Yes, she was President Franklin Roosevelt's wife," said Mrs. White.

"Was your husband handsome?" asked Rosie.

"Rosie, aren't you interested that Mrs. White was friends with Eleanor Roosevelt?" Tess asked in exasperation.

"I'm more interested that she was married to Charles," said Rosie.

"I love the look of old letters," said Lily, running her fingers over an envelope. "I save letters in my wicker trunk."

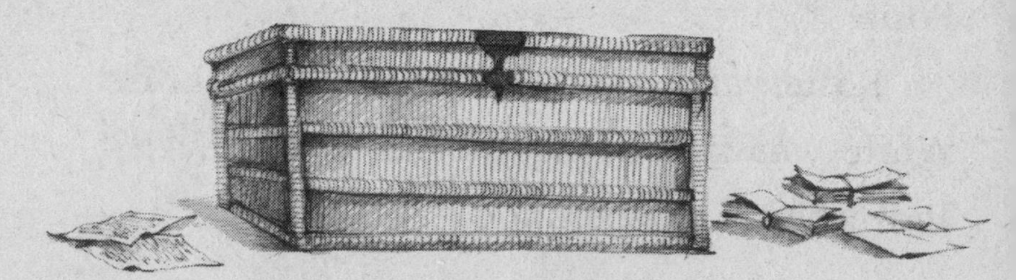

"Oh, yes, save your special letters, dear," said Mrs. White. "When you are as old as I am, you will open them and it will be like reading a novel about someone. So many small, wonderful memories you will have forgotten.

"That's why I've kept Eleanor's letters." Mrs. White smiled. "No matter her place in history, she was my friend, and I love having her voice in my trunk."

"'Voices in the Trunk,'" said Lily. "What a perfect title."

"It will be years before I grow up and get really good letters from people," said Tess.

"Well, you could keep a diary," said Mrs. White. "You can be your own voice for now."

"A diary!" said Lily. "We cousins should keep a diary *together*, of our year in Aunt Lucy's attic!"

"Okay!" said Rosie.

"Great!" said Tess.

On their way home from Mrs. White's house, the girls stopped at a stationery shop and put their money together to buy a small blue diary.

"We'll call it *The Blue Book*," said Lily.

That evening in The Playground, dressed and ready for bed, the girls opened up the book and wrote on its first page:

My name is Lily, I am nine years old and I LO♡e words. Tonight we baked fresh bread with dinner and I called it "celestial." Aunt Lucy said that was a perfect word.

I'm TeSS, today I WORe my RED velveT Beret, which makes me Look EUROPEAn. I Love to sing.

This is Rosie, Our attic is beautiful. It has a high ceiling and a stained-glass window, and we can see the lights downtown at night. I love it here. Good-bye.

"'Good-bye?'" said Tess. "It sounds like you're leaving home."

"Oh," said Rosie. "Maybe I should have said 'Go in peace.'"

And Lily and Tess giggled and giggled while Rosie smiled.

SOLSTICE SUPPER

Michael has invited all of us to his apartment for winter solstice," said Aunt Lucy as she handed out carrot muffins the next morning.

"What's winter solstice?" asked Tess.

"It's the first day of winter and the shortest day of the year," said Aunt Lucy, now passing around boiled eggs. "Michael says he likes to celebrate it with thick, earthy food and cider. A bit like animals fattening up for the cold."

"Ugh," said Tess. "I hope he isn't going to serve worm soup."

"And grub bread," giggled Lucy.

"And beetle bonbons," added Rosie.

Everybody laughed.

"I promise to tell him not *too* earthy," Aunt Lucy said, smiling.

"We should do something for Michael, too,"

said Lily, leaning down to pet Elliott, who had just walked in. "Like a Winter Solstice Reading."

"And a Winter Solstice Song," added Tess.

"How about pastry puffs?" asked Rosie.

"What kind of song is that?" said Tess.

"It's not a song, silly. I mean real pastry puffs," said Rosie. "I could bake some. I saw them in a magazine."

"All of those things sound wonderful," said Aunt Lucy, refilling juice glasses.

"I'm sure Michael would love it."

"Great!" said Tess. "I'll start thinking of a song."

"And I'll write a good read-aloud poem," Lily said. "Something snowy."

"And I'll visit Mr. French!" said Rosie.

At Mrs. White's house that afternoon, the cousins told her of their invitation to Michael's dinner.

"Would you like to come with us, Mrs. White?" asked Rosie. "I'm sure you'd be welcome."

"Thank you, dear, but I try to stay indoors when the weather turns cold. My age, you know," said Mrs. White.

"Do you mind staying inside all the time?" asked Lily. She was sewing the last few stitches around a pretty ivory pillow.

"No, surprisingly, I don't," said Mrs. White. "I have so much to think about."

"Ninety years' worth!" said Rosie.

Mrs. White smiled.

"Yes," she said. "I'm rather like the old cat across the street who sits in the window all day."

"She's probably thinking about all the mice she caught," said Rosie.

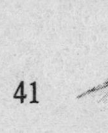

Mrs. White smiled again.

"You girls go on to Michael's and have a good time. And please tell him hello for me."

"We will," Tess promised.

And, as promised, when Michael opened his apartment door on the evening of winter solstice, the first thing the cousins said—in unison—was, "Mrs. White says 'Hello'!"

Michael gave a slight jump, then grinned.

"Did she say it that loud?" he asked.

"That was me," said Tess, stepping through the door. "Singers have to *project*."

"Well, tell her hello back, will you?" said Michael.

"Sure," said Tess. "And I'll tone it down next time."

Aunt Lucy handed Michael a small package. "Something for winter," she said.

"I have something for you, too," Michael answered. "I have something for each of you."

"You got us presents?" asked Lily. "We didn't know about presents. We didn't bring you anything."

"I thought you brought me a poem," said Michael.

"Oh yes, I guess I did," said Lily.

"And I thought you brought me a song," Michael said, looking at Tess.

"Definitely," she answered.

"And Rosie," said Michael, "I sure hope those are pastry puffs in that pan."

Rosie grinned.

"And they're delicious!" she said.

"Well then," said Michael. "You've brought presents after all. And besides, mine for you are quite small."

"Can we open them now?" asked Tess. Lily poked her for her bad manners, but Tess just grinned.

"Let's eat first," said Michael. "The stew's just ready."

"Okay," said the cousins. They hung up their coats and followed Michael and Aunt Lucy into the dining room.

"Wow!" said the cousins.

At the end of the long table, Michael had placed two candelabra full of gold candles flickering in the dim light. The table itself was covered with a paisley cloth and large white plates and mugs and gold-plated silverware.

And in the table's center was a beautiful topiary tree in the shape of . . .

"A rabbit!" said Lily, who loved rabbits.

"It's a hare, actually," said Michael. "It seemed to remind me of snow and survival."

"I love it," said Aunt Lucy. "It's one of the prettiest things I've ever seen."

"It's yours," said Michael. "I made it for your shop window, if you like."

"Michael, really?" said Aunt Lucy, grabbing his hand. "Oh, thank you so very much. I do love it."

"How long did it take you to grow the tree?" asked Rosie.

"Well, I started it quite small, about five years ago," said Michael.

"You didn't know then that you would meet *us* someday," said Rosie with a grin.

"No," said Michael. "But I hoped it." He blushed and glanced at Aunt Lucy.

Suddenly Rosie's stomach growled. She grabbed it as everyone laughed.

"I think that was the dinner bell," said Michael. "Let's eat."

Everyone sat down and Michael dished out the warm, earthy food he had promised: hot chicken stew with potatoes and carrots, baked acorn squash drizzled with melted white cheese, thick slices of farmer's bread spread with butter, and warm rice pudding.

"This is all so good, no one will want my pastry puffs," said Rosie, taking another slice of bread.

"Don't count on it," said Michael. "I'm reserving a space just for that."

"Me too," said Tess.

"Tea and a puff will be perfect after this good meal," said Lily.

"Let's do the poem and song right after dinner," Rosie said. "And then we can have dessert."

"Great," agreed Michael.

The girls helped Michael and Aunt Lucy carry all the dishes and bowls to the kitchen, then everyone settled into Michael's living room.

The girls loved this room. It had a very high ceiling and long, elegant windows, and Michael had filled the room with enormous green plants and trees. It seemed so exotic.

Tess sang her song first. She had chosen a tune called "See You at Suppertime" and, before singing, she put on a yellow bowler hat and a tie and grabbed Michael's umbrella from the corner for added effect.

Everyone loved the song and clapped and whistled when she bowed.

Then Lily stood up. "I wrote a poem I thought would be perfect for winter," she said. And she read:

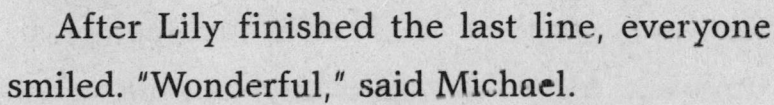

The winter moon is large and white,
The winter snow is soft and light.
Winter trees are bare and brown, and
Winter birds are settling down.
Winter rabbits curl up tight,
Winter bugs all say good night.
Winter winds blow deep and cold, as
Winter stories all are told.
I love winter, quiet and deep.
Winter's here ... the earth's asleep.

After Lily finished the last line, everyone smiled. "Wonderful," said Michael.

"Beautiful," said Aunt Lucy.

"I love good poems," Rosie said.

"It was so good, it made me hungry," said Tess. "Where are those puffs?"

Michael made tea—one of his usual strange concoctions, this time called Cinnamon Oolong Maple Zing. And Rosie handed out the pastry puffs on little saucers.

"Mmmm," said Aunt Lucy, taking a bite. "Perfectly perfect."

"Thank you," Rosie said, grinning.

Once the puffs were eaten, Michael finally gave each cousin her little gift.

"Oh, my goodness!" said Lily. "A pink velvet rabbit for my collection! Thank you, Michael!"

"Look!" said Rosie, unwrapping her gift.

"A stained-glass butterfly! It's *beautiful*! Thank you!"

"I can't believe it," said Tess. "Michael, where did you ever find a poster of *The King and I*? I love it!"

Michael smiled proudly at all the girls.

"And don't forget there's something for you, too, Michael," said Aunt Lucy, pointing to her little package on the table.

Michael carefully unwrapped it. Inside was a book.

"Oh, this is incredible," he said, opening it slowly and examining the pages.

"A book on cacti, published in 1910," said Aunt Lucy. "Aren't the illustrations beautiful?"

"I'm overwhelmed," said Michael.

"It's perfectly perfect," said Tess.

And the cousins grinned as Michael leaned over and kissed Aunt Lucy's cheek.

"I like winter solstice better than any other day of the year," said Tess.

"Short but sweet," said Lily.

"Just like us!" added Rosie.

And when the girls went back home to their attic, they opened up The Blue Book and wrote all about it!